Totally Taylor!

Hanson's Heartthrob

D1111746

Totally Taylor!

Hanson's Heartthrob

by Michael-Anne Johns

SCHOLASTIC INC.
New York Toronto London Auckland Sydney

Photo credits:

front cover: Ernie Paniccioli/Retna
back cover: Evan Agostini/Gamma Liaison

ISBN 0-590-02449-3

12 11 10 9 8 7 6 5 4   8 9/9 0 1 2/0

Printed in the U.S.A.

First Scholastic printing, January 1998

Thanks to the Scholastic superteam —
Craig Walker, Bonnie Bader
and Kristin Earhart — for their support,
sense of humor, and patience.

Contents

Totally Taylor!

Hanson's Heartthrob

"You have to know what you want and keep going for it." – Taylor Hanson, *BOP*

1
Taylor — Heartthrob from the Heartland

In the 1960s, the Beatles had Paul
McCartney....
In the 1970s, the Jackson 5 had little
Michael....
In the 1980s, Duran Duran had John
Taylor....
In the 1990s, the New Kids on the Block
had Joey-Joe McIntire!

All of the above were labeled the "cute one"
and "the sigh-guy" of their mega-music
groups. Paul had those soulful eyes. Michael
had a sweet voice and was a dynamic dancer.
John had that cool hairstyle and his "groovin'"
guitar moves. And Joey, the "baby" of his group,
had bigger-than-big vocals. All of these guys
stood out among their bandmates when on

stage. They were the ones the reporters rushed to first for a quote or comment. They were the ones who seemed to have the most "I Love You" signs held up in the audiences that crowded the stadiums and concert halls where they appeared.

Well, it seems the 1990s now has its heartthrob to sigh for and die for! Jordan Taylor Hanson, otherwise known as Taylor, or Tay, the middle brother of the group Hanson who took "MMMBop" to the top!

Of course, Hanson's seventeen-year-old Isaac and twelve-year-old Zac have their share of fans, fan mail, and cyber-mail. But it's Taylor who's been dubbed the "Heartthrob from the Heartland" in teen magazines and music industry tabloids.

Taylor's Roots

So how did fourteen-year-old Taylor Hanson steal the hearts of half the female population of the world? Well, the story, of course, starts back in his hometown of Tulsa, Oklahoma. Back to the late 1960s in Tulsa, to be exact. That was when two young Nathan Hale High School students, Diana Lawyer and Walker Hanson, met and fell in love. These two young Oklahomans loved their high school years together; they enjoyed learning and participating in extracurricular activities, especially the drama club. They co-starred in quite a few school musical productions and after graduation they went off to the University of Oklahoma together. In 1973, their freshman year at college, the two nineteen-year-olds married. Walker went on to earn a degree and soon joined Helmerich & Payne, Inc., a Tulsa-based international oil drilling company. Eventually he was named the Manager of International Administration.

In 1980, Walker and Diana's first child, Clarke Isaac, was born. He was followed by Taylor, Zachary, daughters Jessica and Avery, and youngest son, Mackenzie.

Early on, the Hansons decided to home-school their children. In an interview with *Entertainment Weekly*, Walker explained that, "We just felt it was better for the kids." It definitely worked out when Walker's position with the oil drilling company relocated the family to Venezuela, Ecuador, and Trinidad-Tobago for a year-long stint. Diana continued her double-duty as mom and teacher, and the family views that year as a very special one. Already close-knit, being away from extended family, friends, and all things familiar made them appreciate each other even more. There were no trips to the local mall for an afternoon of video games or even an instant decision to grab a burger at the local fast-food joint. The Hanson clan had to provide their *own* entertainment during that year, and that's when the group's "legend" began.

Making Music

By now, anyone who is a Hanson fan knows Ike, Taylor, and Zac spent that south-of-the-border year listening to the Time/Life records Walker brought along. The series covered rock 'n' roll songs from 1957 through 1969. The boys spent hours listening to rock 'n' roll legends such as Otis Redding, Chuck Berry, Bobby Darin, the Beach Boys, and Aretha Franklin. Even back then, the boys were beginning to harmonize along with the records. It was just for fun and to pass the time.

When the family returned to Tulsa in 1991, Ike, Taylor, and Zac turned their recreational harmonies into an act. First they called themselves "The Hansons" and then they changed it to the "Hanson Bros." When they found themselves mistakenly being called the "Handsome Brothers," they decided to change it to HANSON. That was the *easy* part. The hard part was getting known. But the *entire* Hanson family took that as a major undertaking.

At first, Hanson was an *a cappella* (without instrumental accompaniment) group and they performed at Walker's company events, friends' parties, community and church productions, state fairs, and even at local amusement parks. Soon they had a large group of fans and Diana started a newsletter to let everyone know the next place Hanson was going to appear. Before they knew it, they had a thriving and ever-growing fan club. In 1992, Hanson made their first appearance at Tulsa's annual arts festival, Mayfest. By 1996, their annual appearance at Mayfest turned into a high point of the festival's concert series.

According to Terry Grufik, the programming director of Tulsa's Performing Arts Center and the man who put together the Mayfest Community Stage event where Hanson appeared: "Anytime they would perform for me at this festival, the area was just covered with little girls. They had quite a fan club, sent out newsletters and things like that. They did quite a bit of self promotion."

When Hanson appeared at their last Mayfest in 1996, they had no idea the next year would bring incredible changes, both personally and professionally. But it did. They met and signed with managers Chris Sabec and Stirling McIlwaine. Sabec admitted in an *Entertainment Weekly* interview he was taking a big chance signing a preteen pop group in the day and age of Nirvana, Pearl Jam, and Alanis Morissette. "I had friends telling me, 'Dude, don't do it — don't embarrass yourself,'" Sabec recalls. But even after fourteen major label turn-downs, he persisted in trying to get them signed because he truly believed in Hanson and their music.

Somehow Sabec convinced Mercury Records executive Steve Greenberg to check Hanson out at the Kansas State Fair. Before they could say, "We're not in Kansas anymore," Greenberg signed Hanson to a six-album deal!

Middle of Nowhere, Hanson's first major label album, went multi-platinum within months of its May 1997 release. Its first single, "MMM-Bop," rode the Number One spot on top of the charts for four weeks, and it was followed by hit singles "Where's the Love" and "I Will Come for You."

By late 1997, the Hanson engine had been tuned-up to high gear. Scheduled to be released before the end of the year were an official Hanson autobiography, a Christmas album entitled *Snowed In*, and a feature-length documentary video called *Tulsa, Tokyo, and the Middle of Nowhere*. Writer-director Morgan J. Freeman, the Sundance Festival winner for the film *Hurricane Streets*, and director David Silver worked on *Tulsa, Tokyo, and the Middle of Nowhere*. Both men worked closely with Taylor, Ike, and Zac on this project, and they only had great things to say about their experience.

Writer Freeman explained to *Entertainment Weekly*, "[*Tulsa, Tokyo, and the Middle of*

8

Nowhere] is not a biopic, but something true to their reality right now, while keeping it tongue-in-cheek."

Director Silver added, "Despite their busy schedule, Hanson found time to participate in the editing process. Their analysis of the footage was absolutely right on."

Taylor in the Spotlight

So it looks as if books, a documentary, a hit CD, top-ranked videos, a "Where's your mustache" milk ad, and a planned 1998 major city tour has solidified Hanson as an American pop icon. But somehow the spotlight shines brightest on Taylor. Perhaps because he seems to be the ultimate "boy next door," the boy who could be the perfect boyfriend or best friend.

If that is really true, Taylor insists it's all because of his parents and his family. "We're really lucky to have the parents that we do," he told *Spin* magazine. To *YM* magazine, Taylor explained, "You really need somebody to help you out." Then, showing off one of his most endearing qualities — a good sense of humor — he added, "Who else is going to carry all the instruments to the stage?!"

And Mr. and Mrs. Hanson are very proud of their boys. Take what happened backstage at the MTV Movie Awards. Before the ceremony, hordes of reporters surrounded the Hanson clan as they hung out with stars like Jim Carrey, Cameron Diaz, Will Smith, and Tyra Banks. A reporter from *Spin* magazine tagged along with Walker Hanson, and the proud papa was overheard explaining the *special* bond the family has with each other. "If you spend all your spare hours working on your golf game, what do you have to show for it in forty years?" asked Walker. "Nothing is more important than the time you spend with your kids."

One person who saw the family bond "up close and personal" was Tamra Davis, the director of the Hanson videos "MMMBop" and "Where's the Love." Her impressions of the entire Hanson family are very perceptive.

"The family is so interesting and rare," she explained. "It's really amazing to work with these kids — and their family. Their mom and dad and their other siblings were very much around. You saw their really strong family unit. The thing that completely amazed me is that they don't criticize each other, they don't fight with each other. I come from a family of four kids and we were always fighting, poking, and teasing each other. It was unbelievable. These kids wouldn't make the others feel insecure. They actually support each other. These kids were so loving of each other, so supportive of each other. I definitely credit their parents in raising them like that."

These solid values have helped make Taylor the focused, confident, and dedicated teenager he is today. And it is these qualities that have made him the unofficial leader of Hanson. Even during their early Mayfest appearances, Terry Grufik recalls, "It was the middle brother, Taylor, who would get them back to business after a break."

In recent interviews, it is Taylor who calms Zac down when he gets a little too excited or shoots Ike a look when one of his cartoon character imitations has gone on a minute too long. Indeed, it is Taylor who has usually taken the lead in the tons of interviews the group has done since *Middle of Nowhere* was released. And it is Taylor who often explains their music and how they came up with an idea for a song.

But don't think for a minute that Taylor is *all* work and no play! No way! Taylor is not above goofing off with his brothers — especially when they are trying to let off steam after whirlwind promotional appearances. Taylor admitted to *BIG!* magazine, "We were thrown out of a toy store recently. They had a display of really bouncy balls and we were allowed to try them out. We ended up bouncing them all over the shop and off the ceiling. All the store assistants kept telling us to calm down. In the end, we were asked to leave. What did they expect us to do? Not throw balls after they had asked us to?"

Right! After all, boys will be boys. They have to do *something* with all that pent-up energy. And when Taylor is back home, there's plenty of ways to burn up some steam. First of all, there is a tree house that the boys built in their backyard. There is also a half-pipe skating ramp in the backyard where you can often find Taylor perfecting his jumps and spins hour after hour. Taylor always takes his blades with him — even on tour — and has reportedly been "caught" blading down the carpeted halls of four-star hotels in Europe, Japan, and Australia!

When it comes time to putting in rehearsal hours at home, Taylor knows how to create the right atmosphere. "We turned our garage in our house into our studio," Taylor told an Australian radio reporter as he described their home work space. "We have a huge mural of things we've drawn. There are drawings that we have done all over the walls."

Drawings? That's right! Taylor is very artistic. In fact, all the brothers have an artistic side. When Hanson was recording their second self-produced CD, *MMMBop*, in Louis Drapp's Tulsa studio, the producer recalled that during breaks the boys would just chill and draw pictures. "They all draw," he explained. "The cool thing about the CD [*MMMBop*] that they did here is the cover. When you open it up, there's a two-page inside folder and it's just artwork from the kids. Really cool. Taylor really liked to draw intricate things like dinosaurs and stuff like that . . . dinosaurs and pictures of the band."

Things haven't changed so much in the past few years. Taylor still loves to draw and you can be sure his art supplies are one of the first things he packs when getting ready to go on the road. Of course, that goes hand in hand with his journal that he always keeps with him. In it, Taylor jots down his memories, his impressions of things that have happened, phrases that might work as a song title, ideas that come to him twenty-four hours a day. His drawings . . . his journals . . . they are all part of the creative Taylor, the young man who has written, with his brothers, hundreds of songs.

That's who Jordan Taylor Hanson is — a fourteen-year-old who never really thought of music as a career. "I just knew I loved music and that it was part of me," he told Richard Wilkins of Australia's *Today Show*. "Whether I did it on a large scale or not, [I knew] it was gonna be part of [my life]."

But once Taylor made the decision to make music his career, he approached it with one of the rules of life he learned from his parents: If you really want something, you have to work for it.

"It's a lot of work, and you have to be really dedicated," Taylor explained to *BOP* magazine when they asked how Hanson exploded onto the music scene with such a blast. "When you want something, it's not that easy. You have to know what you want and keep going for it."

"How much better a job could you possibly have than to be in a band for your whole life?" – Taylor Hanson, *US*

2
Music Man

"Before we learned our instruments," Taylor told a *Spin* magazine writer, "we had this thing back in Tulsa where we'd start to sing in every restaurant we'd go to hoping they'd give us free pizza or something."

That definitely was a modest beginning for a group whose major label debut CD broke the Top Five spot only weeks after its release, a group whose first single, "MMMBop," knocked the Spice Girls off the top of the Pop Chart, a group whose official Web site draws more than 100,000 hits a day.

But the fact of the matter is that *music* has always been a part of them. Taylor says they grew up with homegrown music all around them. During their college years, Diana and Walker Hanson had toured with several gospel groups, and Tay told *Live* magazine, "Our mother was always singing around the house. It's kind of in our genes."

When Hanson visited the office of *Teen Beat* magazine, Taylor explained, "Our parents really introduced us to music. Like our mom really liked Billy Joel and she'd say, 'Here guys, listen to this — it's classic.' Aside from gospel, one of the first songs we ever sang together was Billy Joel's '[For] the Longest Time.'"

Taylor also remembers that the year the family spent in South America helped shape their musical tastes. It was hard being in a strange land with a strange language. Though the boys picked up quite a bit of Spanish during their stay in Venezuela and Ecuador, things that they took for granted back home weren't so easy. "We couldn't understand what people were saying on the radio, so we [listened to] the Time/Life records and all the old songs from the 1950s and early 1960s," Taylor told a *Freezone* reporter.

Through these records, Taylor and his brothers learned a lot about rock 'n' roll. And this knowledge definitely impressed the music industry powers-that-be, from the executives at Mercury Records to amazed music writers. Though the initial reaction for many was to compare Hanson with put-together groups like the Partridge Family, the Monkees, and even New Kids on the Block, those who took the time to *really* listen to their songs walked away with another impression.

Taylor was always confident that would happen. "People are going to say, 'Oh, they're young kids, they don't play, they don't write, they were put together, something's got to be screwy about that,'" Taylor was quoted in the very first *Billboard* article about Hanson. "But you just have to listen to it. The music speaks for itself."

Mercury Records executive Steve Greenberg listened to the music and he told the *Billboard* reporter: "Many people who have dealt with kids on records have taken a fairly condescending approach and made very young-sounding records without a great deal of musical credibility. The music that the Hansons had written demanded greater care than that. The producers we recommended to them were incredibly creative and attuned to what was going on. A lot of the excitement about the album comes from the fact that these classic-style songs are produced in a totally contemporary fashion."

Even music writer Jonathan Gold, who spent the MTV Movie Awards evening with Hanson, was impressed by the group — especially Taylor. In his *Spin* article, he wrote: ". . . Taylor Hanson is extraordinary — able, for instance, to play the tambourine completely without irony, an art that most people thought the Partridge Family had killed off for good. And he can growl

19

through a chorus — admittedly, in a way more reminiscent of Leon Russell than of Otis Redding — without rolling his eyes. On 'Where's the Love,' his high, soulful voice inflects the lyrics with the authority of a gospel singer and the wiggle of a young Stevie Wonder."

What a Voice!

There have been some people who have wondered how long Taylor's high, soulful voice will last. Taylor is fourteen years old and that's about the age when a boy's voice changes. But Taylor assured his fans in *Request* magazine: "Actually, my voice is pretty much done changing. It was pretty bad when we were making the album. If you listen to 'Look at You,' my voice is a couple of notes lower than 'MMMBop.' Or listen to our earlier albums [self-produced *Boomerang* and *MMMBop*]. Isaac sounds a lot like I do now. I sound like Zac and Zac sounds like a Chipmunk. But that's cool. It means the band will change its sound naturally."

Music Is Fun!

What also comes naturally to Taylor and his brothers is their approach to their music. To them, music is just something they grew up loving. Music makes them feel good and that's what they want to share with the rest of the world.

"For a while, there was that alternative thing, and it was huge," Taylor explained to *Entertainment Weekly* about the current music scene. "And now it's coming back to music being fun. Not *corny*, but enjoyable. Not down-and-out 'I hate my life.'"

And just how do Taylor and his brothers come up with their ideas for the songs they write? It just comes naturally, insists Taylor. "It's all part of the package," he said in an Australia TV interview. "Writing songs is just part of it. We don't, you know, ever think about it and say, 'Let's write a cool song.' You just go and do it."

"Anything you're thinking about, you write about," Taylor explained another time when he was talking to a writer for Scholastic magazines. "It's really hard to create a formula because every person has different thoughts, every person has different methods."

In the end, Hanson's songs are definitely a collaborative effort with Taylor, Ike, and Zac all participating. Believe it or not, the beautiful love song "Lucy" is really about the cartoon series *Peanuts*.

"Zac is Schroeder," Taylor confessed to *Rolling Stone*. Not one to remain silent, Zac jumped in with his explanation: "You know how Schroeder's like, 'Lucy, get off of me'? I'm doing the part of Schroeder. And how he's saying, 'Lucy, get off my back,' and he regrets it, and, in the end, he really liked her."

Taylor also explained to the rock magazine how they sometimes let the lyrics almost write themselves. "[In 'Madeline'] we had a chorus of 'Here we go, here we go, around again,' and it sounded better with a name," he said.

The point is that even though they're young, Taylor, Ike, and Zac are true musicians, respected by their fans as well as their peers. So who could ask for any more?

Not Taylor Hanson — he's doing exactly what he wants to do. That's why you have to believe what he told *Smash Hits* magazine when they asked if Hanson's good-time, positive image was real. "Being serious is so boring," he laughed. "Anyone can act like Oasis — what's the point? You can do that anytime, in any job. We love music. It's what we love to do. So we like having fun!"

Jordan Taylor Hanson – a total heartthrob!

Hanson performing at the Arthur Ashe Kids' Day at the Arthur Ashe Tennis Stadium in Flushing, New York.

Taylor is always singled out as the unofficial leader, the backbone and heart of the group.

Outside *The Today Show* in New York City

Music is something Taylor grew up loving.

Taylor was amazing when he played the bongos on *The Late Show With David Letterman*...

. . . and he was awesome on the keyboards, too!

Alan Singer

Roger Glazer

Taylor signing an autograph for a lucky fan.

Zac, Ike, and Taylor pose for the camera in New York City.

Rehearsing for an MTV promo

Taylor and his brothers meet the press!

"We're best friends," Taylor told *Teen Dream* magazine. "We genuinely enjoy hanging out with each other."

David Tonge/Retna

"Being serious is so boring," Taylor told *Smash Hits* magazine.

Youri Lenquette/Retna

Taylor just sits there looking *so* cute as Zac takes the mike, and Ike enjoys a glass of milk at FOX Studios in New York City.

Tay and his brothers took "MMMBop" to the top!

"[Success] can't go to your head," Taylor told a reporter from Australia's Channel 2. "You have to have fun with it, but you can't let it make you any different."

"There's a whole package . . . three brothers who enjoy hanging out with each other, who love what they are doing. That's just who we are. We're just normal guys having fun." –Taylor Hanson, *USA Weekend*

3
Brother-2-Brother

Isaac, Taylor, and Zac have been performing together as a group since 1991 — and that doesn't include their spontaneous harmonies for friends and families before that. In fact, they don't just perform together, they do practically everything together — their music, their home-schooling, their playtime. It's definitely 24–7 for the boys, and, for some, that might create a tense situation. But not for Hanson. The boys really enjoy being together. During a photo shoot in New York City's Central Park, Taylor explained how the three keep it harmonious on and off the stage. "We're basically best friends," he told a *Seventeen* writer.

Continuing that thought with *Rolling Stone*, Taylor said, "Being in a band together makes it even better, because we know each other so well. It's like, you're gonna argue, then it's over, and you're still together. What are you gonna do? Walk across the room and pout?"

Putting in his two cents, Ike summed it up with, "You still gotta rehearse."

Of course, Ike, Taylor, and Zac are hardly little angels *all* the time. They *do* have their moods and their arguments with each other. "We truly enjoy each other's company," Ike told *Teen Dream* magazine. "We do fight, which is only normal for brothers. But it's basically all in fun."

That's right! Instead of knockdown fights or shouting matches, they usually resolve any conflict with a sense of humor. As a matter of fact, they approach almost *everything* with a wink and a joke — especially in interviews, when they are asked about their relationship with each other.

They've been known to reveal secrets (and lies) about each other during interviews — especially if it will get a laugh. How about the time during an MTV interview/*Seventeen* photo shoot that Ike stopped everything to tell Taylor to blow his nose? "Why?" Taylor asked. "Just so you know, your nose is running," Ike explained in his best big-brother voice as Tay sniffed and snuffled away!

And then there was the time an Australian interviewer was pressing the boys about how much money they were making. He kept probing and prodding. "Are you rich?" he asked. Taylor quickly responded, "That's kind of a weird question because the thing is *that's* not what it's all about at all." When the reporter pressed on, Zac jumped in with a total conversation stopper. "You have big eyebrows!" he said to the interviewer, and, after a beat or two, everyone cracked up laughing!

The brothers can talk forever. Sometimes an interviewer loses control of the chat and the boys practically take over. Here's an example of a back-and-forth moment during their first interview for England's BBC:

BBC: Ike, can you introduce us to . . .

Zac: . . . Tell us his age, what he does, what he's like . . .

Ike: OK, well, that is Zac. Zac, say hi.

Zac: Hi!

Ike: He is eleven and he plays the drums.

BBC: And his nickname is Animal, right?

Ike: Yes, his nickname is Animal, from the Muppets. Exactly.

BBC: Because he's just wild?

Ike: He's just crazy.

BBC: Zac, introduce us to Taylor.

Zac: Taylor is the piano player. He is fourteen and he is more [of a] perfectionist as far as vocals go.

BBC: And Taylor, introduce us to Isaac. What's he do?

Taylor: Ike is the guitar player and many

more things. He sings and he's sixteen and he's awesome and he does everything.

What about the time the boys were talking to *Sugar* magazine and got on the topic of how some people say the Hansons look like girls?!

> **Zac:** We're the long-haired guys that look like girls!
>
> **Taylor:** Yeah, we seem to get the "girls" comment pretty frequently.
>
> **Isaac:** I guess people just take a look at the back of our heads, and make an assumption.
>
> **Zac:** But then we turn round to face them and they go, "YEEAAARRGH!"
>
> **Taylor:** Yeah, they go, "That's just the ugliest woman I've ever seen!"

Or, how about the interview Hanson did with an Australian DJ named Ugly Phil? Zac actually had been laid-back during the first part of the interview, and the DJ asked why he'd been so quiet.

> **Phil: Feel free to say anything at anytime you feel like it, Zac, you know . . .**
>
> **Taylor:** He's just sitting there giving you the, like, angry stare!

Ike: Yeah, the evil eye . . .

Phil: I know, I didn't mean what I said about drummers being silly. . . .

Ike: Yeah, [Zac], he didn't mean it. And [Zac's] still quiet!!

Zac: [In a pretend evil voice] Well, you're gonna die. . . . [Zac, Tay, and Ike all get up and do karate moves and make punching noises!]

Phil: It's the Anti-Zac!!! Oh, my gosh!!!

As the little brother, Zac might sometimes be overlooked — *if* he weren't in a group called Hanson. Actually Zac is the most vocal — and sometimes the most frantic — of the brothers. But the love he feels for his older brothers is always obvious. "We'd never consider making music separately," he told *Teen Dream*, "because we've been together all our lives."

Of course, it is Zac who in an early interview admitted to *Smash Hits* magazine: "We goof off [together]. We like to, say, climb up on a roof and drop water bombs on people. Stuff like that!"

When Zac stopped revealing embarrassing water-bomb secrets, he did confide to the British magazine reporter the truth about Hanson's brotherly love. "I guess I need looking after sometimes," Zac admitted. "We look after each other, but I don't *need* baby-sitting. I don't think of those two as older than me. I think they're eleven as well. To Tay, we're all fourteen, and to Ike, we're all sixteen, I guess. . . . I don't think of them as big brothers. They're like my best friends. Only bester!"

In response to Zac's observation, Taylor interjected, "It usually ends up with Zac looking after us!" But after a moment of thought, he added, "It's great to be good friends with your brothers. Then you've got friends for life."

And what about the young Hanson siblings? Are they being groomed to follow in Ike, Taylor, and Zac's footsteps? Well, according to Taylor in an article in *US* magazine, nine-year-old Jessica, six-year-old Avery, and three-year-old Mackenzie ". . . know what's going on. They'll sit in on conversations with the label about artwork on the record and photo shoots, and my sister will go, 'Why did the manager do that? He should have done this.' Or, 'You guys are squinting too much in this picture. Your hair is cool, but we can't see your eyes.'"

According to Zac, little brother Mackie could give him a run for his money given enough time and opportunity. Laughingly — and a little bit seriously — Zac told *Rolling Stone*: "Mackie — he's got the rhythm. I've got to watch out. He'll steal my place!"

It looks as if the younger Hanson siblings have a tale or two to tell, too!

"Jessica will see girls freaking out when they meet us, and she'll say, `Girls are weird. Why do they do that?'" – Ike Hanson, *US*

4
Taylor on Girls, Dating and More

"None of us have girlfriends," Taylor admitted to a *Rolling Stone* reporter right around the time "MMMBop" hit the Number One spot on *Billboard*'s Pop Chart. This was a time when Taylor and his brothers were tops on millions of girls' heartthrob lists, but still there were no girlfriends on the horizon.

It's not because they wouldn't love to be going on dates, or to parties and proms, but the fact of the matter is that Ike, Taylor, and Zac just don't have the time to spare for that kind of fun.

Always the instigator, Zac whispered to the *Rolling Stone* writer, "Ike is a girl charmer. He'll always say nice things to girls. It's just something he does."

But Ike explained the difference between being a smooth talker and boyfriend material right now in his career. "It would be wrong for me to have a girlfriend, anyway, at this point in time," he said. "Because I'm, like, gone all the time."

And a young, but wise, Zac added, "For the girl it would be sad."

Taylor, however, has something to add to this topic. He does agree that it's hard to have a serious relationship if you're a young pop star. He doesn't believe that distance makes the heart grow fonder. Just the opposite, in fact. But he's not denying there are times he wishes things could be different.

Of course, there were the recent cyber-rumors flying across the Internet that Taylor really did have a girlfriend, but she was just staying in the background.

"Don't believe everything you log onto," he told *YM* magazine when they brought up the girlfriend story making the rounds on the Web. "I don't have a girlfriend yet," but then he added: ". . . if you live life, you meet girls. That's pretty basic."

Taylor also feels that settling down to a one-on-one relationship with a girl at this point in his life would not only be unfair to her, but to him, also. There are a lot of things he wants to accomplish in his life, and if he had a girlfriend right now, he might not be able to concentrate on and dedicate the amount of time needed to achieve those goals.

Actually, Taylor is a bit surprised at the emphasis and peer pressure put on preteens and young teens to start dating. "I thought you weren't meant to be into girls until you were about fourteen," he observed in a *Smash Hits* article. "But it seems everyone is getting girlfriends younger. What's the point of getting a girlfriend when you're eleven? What do you do? Ring up and go, 'Let's get together and talk.'"

Of course, Taylor may have been directing his "eleven-year-old" comments to his younger brother, but Zac is in total agreement. Even in the very beginning of Hanson, they had frenzied female fans, but Zac giggled to *Spin* magazine about those days: "I was six. What was I going to do with a girl?"

But Taylor really tries to keep things in perspective when it comes to girls. When music video director Tamra Davis worked with Hanson on "MMMBop" and "Where's the Love," she was very impressed with how Taylor kept his mind on work. When they made "MMMBop," they spent time at a couple of public shooting locations. They hadn't released the single yet and Hanson wasn't even known, but somehow word got out that three cute boys were making a video. And somehow bunches of girls appeared at both the beach and blading locations. It was Davis' first experience with Hanson-mania. When Davis joined Hanson in London for the "Where's the Love" shoot, she was used to the crowds the boys drew. But she was surprised at how quickly Taylor was singled out by girls — even women — of all ages!

"Sometimes I think it's good he's not in school," she observed after spending worktime and playtime with the group. "If he were [in school], the girls would never leave him alone, he wouldn't get anything done."

Even more impressive to Davis was Taylor's attitude about being a heartthrob. "He acts like he doesn't even notice it," she laughed. "It's almost like he has no idea!"

When his "teen idol" status is pointed out to Taylor, he tries to ignore it. "You have to be thankful to everybody who appreciates your music," Taylor told *Request* magazine. "But sometimes it feels like the girls aren't screaming at us; they're screaming at some band called Hanson they saw on TV."

Fan Mania
While the fans may not seem real, sometimes when Hanson is on stage there are times that being too close to fans can be a little bit scary.

Like the Beatles and the New Kids on the Block before them, Hanson has made quite a few mad dashes to the safety of waiting limousines or backstage doors. Though Taylor admits he's always amazed at the enthusiasm fans have when they see Hanson, he'll never forget one of their first post-"MMMBop" release appearances. It was at the Garden State Plaza Mall, in Paramus, New Jersey. Thousands of girls crowded in the area set aside for the Hanson appearance. It took the boys forty-five minutes just to squeeze their way through the crowd to get to the stage area. A *Request* magazine reporter described Hanson's slow trek through the crowd to the stage as "a human carwash." Ike recalled, "Taylor's shirt got ripped and his shoelace snapped. Zac almost got crushed by a sea of people."

Even so, Taylor tries to take this kind of attention in stride. Shortly after the Garden State Plaza Mall experience, he talked to a *Los Angeles Times* writer and observed, "All these screaming girls and guys going crazy . . . you just have to have fun with it."

But sometimes it's not all fun and games. When Taylor is doing something normal — like shopping or going to a movie or hanging out with his friends and an uproar erupts, he's not a happy camper! "I get really embarrassed," he told *BIG!* magazine when asked if he likes being chased by fans. "We were at McDonald's last week and we were waiting to order our food. All of a sudden, there was whispering going up and down the line and people were saying, 'Hanson . . . Taylor . . .' No one said anything to me, they just whispered and I was just standing there. In the end, I got my food and ran out."

So, as normal and typical as Taylor likes to be when he's offstage, he has finally realized he won't be meeting any date-mates in line at McDonald's. He's lucky if he has time to get a burger and large fries before he's mobbed!

Yet, all this attention still hasn't gone to Taylor's head. When asked who's the most popular with the girls in the group, Taylor is the ultimate diplomat. "That's the good thing about us," he fielded the question from the *BIG!* interviewer. "Each of us appeals to different ages. A lot of the younger girls like Zac, although he does get older girls, too!"

"It's great to be good friends with your brothers. Then you've got friends for life." – Taylor Hanson, *Smash Hits*

5
The Tay Q&A

Here are the answers to questions each and every Taylor fan *wants* to and *needs* to know!

Q: What kind of letters and e-mail do you get now that you've had some major hits like "MMMBop" and "Where's the Love"?
Taylor: "We get both sides — the 'Oh, I hate you guys, you stink' side and 'You guys are so awesome,'" Taylor told *Rolling Stone* magazine. "The positive outweighs the negative by far."

Q: How do you feel when someone puts down your music?

Taylor: "Everybody has their opinion," he confided to a reporter for *US* magazine. "That's part of life. It's fine, you know."

Q: What inspired you to start a band?
Taylor: "I don't really know," he answered a fan during an America Online cyber-chat. "It was so natural. We just started singing and knew that's what we wanted to do."

Q: When you write a song, which comes first — the lyrics or the music?
Taylor: "There's really no way to predict how you're going to write a song," he explained to Scholastic magazines. "It's impossible to know how it's [always] going to happen, but I would say music first. That's because the music is what's inspiring you. But a lot of times you never know, like with the song 'Weird' — that was inspired by the word *weird*."

Q: If you went to the moon, what object, person, or animal would you take with you?
Taylor: [He laughed when he answered this question for the British magazine *BIG!*] "I'd say a dog because they're loyal. But then again I might take a monkey like the one in Indiana Jones. The little fella

would be loads of fun. Plus a CD player with tons of CDs."

Q: What's the best piece of advice you've ever heard?
Taylor: "You have to like yourself before you can do anything," he told the *BIG!* interviewer.

Q: Does it scare you that so many people know everything about you now?
Taylor: "You'd be surprised what you *don't* know," he insisted during the AOL chat. "But it gets pretty wild."

Q: What's the best part about being home-schooled?
Taylor: "We couldn't have been the group without doing that, because we were around each other so much. Not to mention, we wouldn't have had the relationship with each other," he told *Rolling Stone* magazine.

Q: Do you feel you missed out on anything by being home-schooled and not going to regular school?
Taylor: "Being home-schooled has let us utilize what we do," he explained to *Teen Beat*. "Home-schooling lets you focus on

things you enjoy," he told *Seventeen* in another interview. "We'll read about [the French cathedral] Notre Dame and then go to Paris to see it." And when Taylor sat down with the British teen magazine *Smash Hits*, he explained the best part about home-schooling. "We've been able to practice [our music] rather than being stuck [in] school and all that," he said. "It's really nice because you can focus on the subjects you really like and are interested in."

Q: How would you describe yourself as compared to your brothers Ike and Zac?
Taylor: "I'm the quietest one, obviously," he told Kurt Loder during an interview with MTV.

Q: How would you describe your relationship with Ike and Zac?
Taylor: "We're best friends," he told *Teen Dream* magazine. "We genuinely enjoy hanging out with each other."

Q: What is "MMMBop" really about?
Taylor: "'MMMBop' is really about friendship," he explained to Kurt Loder. "The first verse says, 'You have so many relationships

in this life/Only one or two will last/You go through all the pain and strife/And you turn your back and they're gone so fast.' And that's what it's really about. It's deeper than it sounds."

Q: You've traveled all over the globe in the past year — what's the coolest place you've been?
Taylor: "If we told you, we'd have to kill you," he joked during a Canadian online chat. "It's top secret."

Q: Do you ever wish you weren't famous so you could spend time with friends and go to parties?
Taylor: "Whatever we do, we make it fun," Taylor explained to another Canadian online chatter. "We meet friends all over the world. It's really cool."

Q: What's the biggest perk of being a pop star?
Taylor: "Getting to see different countries and places," he told Cindy Crawford on an MTV *House of Style* interview. "I think that's been really fun for us."

Q: What's it like being a member of the hottest band? Has it changed you?

Taylor: "I didn't know we were the hottest band," he answered a fan during the AOL chat. "No, it shouldn't change you and it doesn't."

Q: What's the most exhausting day you've spent so far?
Taylor: "We once did twenty-one interviews in one day," Taylor told *Rolling Stone*. But he admits that, "Photo shoots are more exhausting."

Q: Do fans who are overzealous ever scare you?
Taylor: "You get a few, one or two percent, who are maybe a little bit dangerous," Taylor told *Entertainment Weekly*. "There's one guy, maybe, whose girlfriend is in love with you, or he's kind of screwy anyway. But most of them are fans who are just excited."

Q: What was the biggest false rumor you've heard about yourself?
Taylor: "There was one that went around that I got nodules [on my vocal cords]. . . . and another one was in a magazine — that I was dead!" he confessed during a BBC interview in London. "I think it got dramatically exaggerated." Neither are true, of course!

Q: What would you do if you weren't in a band?

Taylor: "I wouldn't be me if [I] didn't sing, you know," he told the BBC reporter. "I'd like to meet somebody who liked me for me, but the music is so us, it's, you know . . . I wouldn't know who I'd be if I didn't do music."

Q: What did you do when "MMMBop" went Number One?

Taylor: "First of all, you just go crazy, because you can never expect that. On MTV we announced that if we got to Number One, we would go to Laser Quest. So we kept our promise and went there with some friends and partied."

Q: When was the last time you cried?

Taylor: "Last time we did an interview!" he kidded with a reporter from the British teen magazine *BIG!* "Do we cry at movies? No, we watch action movies and we don't cry at Arnold Schwarzenegger."

Q: You broke your arm a couple of years ago — how did it happen?

Taylor: "I was going down this huge hill on my bike to see a house my parents were going to buy," he told the *BIG!* reporter.

They were driving up the hill as I was coming down and I saw the car heading towards me. I braked and went straight over the handlebars. I lay in the road while my parents rushed over and picked me up. I looked at my arm and it had just snapped."

Q: Who helped you most in your career?
Taylor: "Our parents," he told an interviewer from Australia's Channel 7 Network. "Without them we probably couldn't have done it because we were so young. It would have been impossible to make it happen." And on another down-under TV show Taylor told the Australian *Today Show* reporter: "Our parents were with us when we were [singing] locally. It's not like, all of a sudden our parents came in and said, 'Yeah, these are our kids — here!' and it started happening. They were there the entire time and have always been there. Our family goes with us everywhere we go — it's just what we do."

Q: How do your friends feel about you being in a pop group?
Taylor: "All of our friends would just die to do what we're getting to do," Taylor told a

Rolling Stone reporter. "A lot of them have never been to New York or Europe or even out of their home state. And we're getting to — not to mention do what we love to do, which is sing."

Q: How do you cope with the stress and adulation that comes along with fame?
Taylor: "Well, you know, whenever we get stressed we just do whatever together — swim in the pool with all our clothes on!" he laughingly told a reporter from Australia's Channel 2 after he, Isaac, and Zac had jumped in a pool on a whim. But on a more serious note, Taylor insisted: "[Success] can't go to your head. You have to have fun with it, but you can't let it make you any different."

Q: Is it true you usually order diet soda when you're on the road?
Taylor: "Yes, we drink it because pop has a lot of sugar, and you know what that means — PIMPLES!" admitted Taylor to *Rolling Stone* magazine.

Q: How does it feel to be compared to the Partridge Family?
Taylor: "I'm stumped there," he laughed

when he answered a fan on the AOL chat. "It's cool to be compared to anybody who was successful. That's the truth."

Q: Are boys better than girls?
Taylor: "That's kind of a dumb question," he responded to a *BIG!* magazine query. "[For example], hardly any girls are in things like violent movies — where hundreds of guys get blown to bits with tons of blood, guts, and stuff flying! Girls just want to talk, they want romance and there's nothing wrong with that!"

"You have to like yourself before you can do anything!" – Taylor Hanson, *BIG!*

6
Taylor's Astro-Chart

Taylor's Birthdate: March 14, 1983
Astrological Sign: Pisces
Pisces Element: Water
Pisces Planetary Ruler: Neptune
Pisces Symbol: The Fish
Pisces Motto: I Believe
Pisces Colors: Mauve, purple, aqua-marine
Pisces Gemstones: White opal, jade, pearl, amethyst

The Pisces Personality

Pisces is one of the most interesting of the Zodiac signs because it represents old age and the wisdom that comes along with it. When a child seems to understand grown-up ideas, adults often say something like, "Oh, he's six going on

53

sixty," or "Out of the mouths of babes . . ." A true believer of astrology sees something else. They usually check out the child's birthday and astrological sign — and very often they discover the child is a Pisces.

According to astrologers, someone who is born under the sign of Pisces is also very sensitive. They are dreamers who understand the creative side of life. They love painting, literature, and music. Pisces are true friends, who will be there for you through thick and thin. They are often generous, mainly because money and material things mean very little to them. Happiness, joy, and inner peace are what Pisces seek out.

On the downside, however, Pisces can be very emotional and sometimes overly sensitive. And sometimes they escape into their fantasies to avoid the harsh realities of everyday life. And because they are such sympathetic listeners, Pisces have to make sure they don't get too far into their friends' problems and not deal with their own lives.

March 14th Pisces Traits

According to many astrologers, those born on March 14 are protective of their families and are often leaders. Independence is another quality they have. They are often outspoken and not afraid to let people know how they feel.

Taylor to a T?

Taylor is definitely there for his siblings. He always takes time to share himself with them, whether it be showing Avery how to draw a flower or working on a chorus with Ike. And whenever anyone describes Hanson, Taylor is always singled out as the unofficial leader, the backbone, and the heart of the group. He, indeed, is the listener, the counselor of the Hanson family.

Other Famous People Who Share Taylor's Birthday:

Frank Borman — Astronaut.
Michael Caine — Actor.
Billy Crystal — Actor and comedian.
Albert Einstein — Nobel Prize–winning physicist and mathematician who is famous for discovering the Theory of Relativity. (Remember the poster of Einstein in the "MMMBop" video?)
Quincy Jones — Music producer, writer, and composer; record company executive.
Hank Ketcham — Cartoonist and creator of *Dennis the Menace.*
Johann Strauss, Sr. — Composer, conductor, and violinist.

By the Numbers

Taylor's birthdate number is 5, which is found by taking the date, 14, and calculating the simple equation 1 + 4 = 5. In numerology, the number 5 is characterized by a resilient and flexible nature, one that can rebound quickly from disappointments and hard knocks, but is also not afraid to try something new. Sounds like Taylor, doesn't it?

Taylor's name number is 1. This is determined by using the chart below:

1	2	3	4	5	6	7	8	9
A	B	C	D	E	F	G	H	I
J	K	L	M	N	O	P	Q	R
S	T	U	V	W	X	Y	Z	

Find the numbers that correspond with the letters in TAYLOR:

T = 2
A = 1
Y = 7
L = 3
O = 6
R = 9

Then add them up until you get a single digit:

2 + 1 + 7 + 3 + 6 + 9 = 28
2 + 8 = 10
1 + 0 = 1

Taylor's name number is 1 and in numerology this signifies a leader! Those with the name number of 1 are usually creative, determined, self-confident, and comfortable in the spotlight. Their independent attitude and approach to life can bring them to the tops of their chosen paths, as well as fame and fortune. Sounds like Taylor, doesn't it?

"Our family's ethnic background is Danish. That explains our love for Lego!"
– Taylor Hanson, YTV-Canada

7
Taylor's Ultimate Fact File

Do you know what color toothbrush Taylor uses? Or what color jellybeans he eats first? Or what school subject is his favorite? If you don't — and even if you do — check out this ultimate, everything-you-need-to-know list on Jordan Taylor Hanson!

GENERAL INFO
Full Name: Jordan Taylor Hanson
Professional Name: Taylor Hanson
Nickname: Tay
Birthday: March 14, 1983
Astro Sign: Pisces
Birthplace: Jenks, Oklahoma, a suburb of Tulsa
Current Residence: Tulsa, Oklahoma
Former Residences: Trinidad-Tobago; Venezuela; Ecuador
Parents: Walker and Diana Hanson
Father's Profession: Until Walker retired to work full-time with Hanson, he was a financial executive for an oil drilling company.
Siblings: Older brother, Isaac; younger

brothers, Zachary and Mackenzie; younger sisters, Jessica and Avery

Pet: A cat named MaMa

Weight: 115 pounds

Height: 5'8"

Hair: Blond

Eyes: Blue

Dimple: When he smiles he has one on his right cheek

Instruments: Keyboards, piano, synthesizer, bongos, tambourine, drums

Band Position: Lead singer and keyboards

Other Talent: Drawing — especially cartoons

First Career Ambition: To be an architect or a cartoonist

Computer: A Toshiba laptop — he loves to surf the Net

Worst Habit: Tapping on everything

Best Quality: He's a perfectionist

Boxers or Briefs: Boxers

Bodyguard: Jason Browning (he's that big guy with the shaved head you always see with Hanson)

FAVES
Color: Red
Second fave color: Blue
Food: Burritos, steak, chicken, fish, cheese-burgers with everything, mashed pota-toes
Condiment: Heinz ketchup — especially on cheeseburgers
Dessert: His mom's brownies
Candy: Jellybeans (especially the cherry-red ones!)
Drinks: Bottled water, Mugs Rootbeer
Ice Cream: Strawberry
Peanut Butter: Creamy (never crunchy!)
Breakfast Cereal: Cocoa Puffs
Fast Food: McDonald's and pizza
L.A. Restaurant: Johnny Rockets
School Subjects: Computer arts and liter-ature
TV Shows: *Friends*, *Frasier*, *Seinfeld*, *Ani-maniacs*
Radio Show: Casey Kasem's Top 40
Music: '60s Motown
Bands: No Doubt, Counting Crows, Phish, Blues Traveler, Spin Doctors
Singers: Alanis Morissette, Billy Joel, Na-talie Merchant, Otis Redding, Chuck Berry

Actor: Tom Cruise

Actress: Jennifer Aniston

Spice Girl: Emma "Baby Spice" Bunton

Movie: *Star Wars*

TV Cartoon Show: "I love *Freakazoid,*" he told *YM* magazine.

Cartoon Characters: Beavis and Butt-Head

Sports: Rollerblading, soccer, go-carting

Game: Laser Quest

Shoes: Adidas, Doc Martens

Clothing: His maroon sports jersey, baggy pants

Store: The Gap

Jewelry: His necklaces — one has a cross, another has a soccer ball, and another has a star in a ring

Shampoo: Flex

Toothpaste: Colgate

Pastimes: Reading and drawing

Childhood Toys: His plastic sword and Legos

Animals: Monkeys and dolphins

Cologne: CK Be

Football Team: Miami Dolphins

Expressions: "That's cool!" and "Weird!"

FASCINATING FACTS

• Along with Isaac and Zac, Taylor built a tree house in their backyard in Tulsa.

• Taylor's toothbrush is aqua.

• When he was a little kid, Taylor never took off his favorite baseball cap.

• Taylor broke his arm in a bicycle accident several years ago — he saved his cast!

• Taylor wears a retainer — that's why he sometimes lisps.

• Taylor and Zac drew the "Muscle Men" cartoon inside the *Middle of Nowhere* CD.

• Taylor keeps a journal and writes in it every day.

• Taylor has a scar on his chin — he got it when he ran into a glass door when he was a little guy.

• Taylor admitted to *BIG!* magazine that he and his brothers are definitely messy — even when they are traveling. "We never keep our rooms clean. We leave clothes everywhere and our skates are always lying on the floor. People always trip over them."

"We read our fan mail – whatever we can. We love reading the mail!"
– Taylor Hanson, YTV-Canada

8
Reach Out
and Touch Taylor!

With Hanson gearing up for a major U.S. tour in 1998, you just may be able to check out Taylor and brothers Isaac and Zac in your own hometown or a town close to you. They plan to appear in dozens of cities and towns across the country, so you might want to start making your concert signs — "I Love Taylor!" . . ."Baby Blue Eyes!" . . ."MMM-Taylor!"

Or, you might want to write Taylor a letter telling him right where you'll be sitting in hopes he'll look in your direction! Here are a few "Dos & Don'ts" to keep in mind when writing Taylor:

- Do keep your letter short and to the point — Taylor doesn't have a lot of time to read ten-page epics!
- Don't put perfume all over your letter — it never smells as nice as you think!

- Do choose a brightly colored envelope — it will catch Taylor's eye when he pores through the thousands of letters he gets every week!
- Don't write a mushy love letter — it embarrasses Taylor!
- Do tell him about yourself — what grade you're in, your favorite hobbies, sports, talents, etc.
- Don't *expect* a personal letter or phone call back from Taylor — if you get one, it will be a pleasant surprise!

Where To Contact Taylor Hanson
Addresses ✳ Fan Clubs ✳ E-mail ✳ Chat Rooms ✳ Web Pages ✳ Cyber-Links

Official Hanson Fan Club:	HITZlist P.O. Box 703136 Tulsa, OK 74170
Record Company:	Taylor Hanson c/o Mercury Records 825 Eighth Avenue New York, NY 10019
Hanson's Hotline:	1-918-446-3979

(Be sure to get a parent's permission!)

Official Web Page:
http://www.hansonline.com

Cool Site:
http://www.hansonhitz.com

Hanson AOL Screenname:
mmmbop@aol.com

Mercury Records Hanson Web Page:
http://www.mercuryrecords.com/mercury/
    artists/hanson/hanson_homepage.html

Fan Club:
http://members.tripod.com/~jenilynn/

"Music was unavoidable in our house." – Taylor Hanson, *YM*

9
Hanson Discography

Albums
(*Original songs by Hanson)

Boomerang (self-released)
"Boomerang"*
"Poison Ivy"
"Lonely Boy"*
"Don't Accuse"*
"Rain"*
"More Than Anything"*
"The Love You Save"
"Back to the Island"
"More Than Anything"* (reprise)

MMMBop (self-released)
"Day Has Come"*
"I'll Be Thinking of You"*
"Two Tears"*

"Stories"*
"River"*
"Surely as the Sun"*
"Something New"*
"MMMBop"*
"Soldier"*
"Pictures"*
"Incredible"*
"With You in Your Dreams"*
"Sometimes"*
"Baby You're So Fine"*
"MMMBop"* (long version)

Middle of Nowhere (Mercury)
"Thinking of You"*
"MMMBop"*
"Weird"*
"Where's the Love"*
"Yearbook"*
"Lucy"*
"I Will Come for You"*
"A Minute Without You"*
"Madeline"*
"With You in Your Dreams"*
"20 Empty Tracks"*
"Man From Milwaukee"* (bonus track)

"Music can't be about the fame or the money or any of that stuff. You really have to love it." – Taylor Hanson, *Teen Beat*

10
75 Must-Know Hanson Facts!

1. Taylor likes to wear a long braid in the back of his hair.
2. Taylor blushes very easily!
3. Together Ike, Taylor, and Zac have written over 300 songs.
4. Though their mother, Diana, has been their home-school teacher for years, they now have a math tutor who even travels with them.
5. Word has it that Ike names his guitars after girls he likes — just like the legendary B.B. King!
6. Ike wears clear braces.
7. Ike, Taylor, and Zac all admit they bite their nails.
8. The first song Ike ever wrote was called

"Rain Falling Down" — he was in the third grade.

9. Zac's favorite soda is Dr Pepper.
10. Back in their home in Tulsa, Ike, Tay, and Zac share a bedroom. Ike and Tay sleep in a bunk bed and Zac has his own bed!
11. Zac admits that sometimes he wears earplugs when they perform because the screams from the audience are so loud.
12. Ike is a *Star Wars* fan.
13. The boys love to relax by playing Ping-Pong.
14. All three boys collect Legos and love to build intricate medieval castles with them.
15. "MMMBop" was filmed in Malibu and Hollywood.
16. Ike, Taylor, and Zac all play the piano.
17. Taylor writes with his right hand and denies he's ambidextrous!
18. At the MTV Movie Awards, baby brother Mackie gave supermodel Elle MacPherson a hug and wouldn't let go!
19. During the video shoot for "Where's the Love," Jessica and Avie kept drawing pictures for director Tamra Davis. She still has them pasted up in her house.
20. When Hanson appeared on MTV's *House of Style,* Zac wanted to go into a body-piercing place. His mom said, "NO WAY!"

21. Word has it that Zac loves the miniature shampoo bottles in the hotels they've stayed in all over the world.
22. Tay has a Kurzweil keyboard.
23. Zac wrote "Man From Milwaukee" when the family van broke down outside Albuquerque — "Milwaukee sounded better than Albuquerque," Zac says.
24. Hanson sang at the opening game of the 1997 World Series between the Cleveland Indians and the Florida Marlins.
25. Taylor uses Flex shampoo.
26. Ike uses Pantene Pro-V.
27. "MMMBop" was nominated for Best New Artist in a Video at the 1997 MTV Video Music Awards — they didn't win.
28. Of the big MTV Music Video Awards winner Jamiroquai, Taylor says: "He's totally into Stevie Wonder, you can tell." Ike adds, "[He's] one of my favorites. The video [for 'Virtual Insanity'] is incredible."
29. In an interview with *BOP* magazine, Zac describes himself in comparison to Ike and Tay, "I'm the weirdo. Those two [Ike and Tay] are normal, so normal people usually stick together, but I'm a Gonzo."
30. Ike told *Entertainment Weekly* that Hanson's ambition was to "keep doing our music whether we sell one record or one million."

31. Ike likes to wear high-top sneakers or hiking boots.

32. Hanson has been offered several TV specials and a cartoon series based on their life. So far, they've turned everything down except for the documentary *Tulsa, Tokyo, and the Middle of Nowhere*.

33. There is an official line of Hanson merchandise including T-shirts, baseball caps, coffee mugs, backpacks, keyrings, and lots more.

34. When Hanson did *The Jenny McCarthy Show* on MTV, the actress ran onto the set and tackled Zac. "But Zac wouldn't let her kiss him!" Ike told *Sugar* magazine.

35. On days off Ike likes to hang out at the mall.

36. Zac's favorite school subject is art.

37. Zac told *YM* that "Ding Dongs and Twinkies are my most important food group. I also like lasagna and hot dogs and pizza. . . ."

38. Ike likes to imitate Kermit the Frog and Beavis and Butt-Head.

39. In the "MMMBop" video, Taylor is "driving" the same car Sandra Bullock did in *Speed 2*.

40. Also in the "MMMBop" video, the skating tumble was very real. "Definitely all real," insists Zac.

41. Hanson posed for their *Seventeen* magazine photo shoot in New York City's Central Park.

42. Ike told *Seventeen*: "We don't want to be the next Partridge Family. Right now we're focusing on the music."

43. Ike got his first guitar from a pawn shop in Tulsa.

44. Tay's first keyboards were borrowed from a friend.

45. Zac found his first drum set in a friend's attic.

46. Zac told *YM*: "I've never kissed a girl. But I do think about it. And it's not like there's just one type of girl who's right for me, because you say that and then you fall for someone who's the exact opposite of what you said."

47. When Hanson was working with the Dust Brothers on *Middle of Nowhere,* Zac took a flying dive into their swimming pool — with his clothes on. "Zac played the drums soaking wet on one song," Taylor laughed in an interview with *Seventeen*.

48. Zac loves action movies.

49. Ike sprained his ankle about a year ago. He was climbing a plum tree and fell down and landed right on his feet!

50. Zac thinks the best phrase is from *Toy Story* — "To infinity and beyond!"

51. Diana Hanson has blonde hair just like her sons — only longer.

52. Walker Hanson has a beard.

53. Zac explained to a reporter that they are not spoiled. "We still do the chores," he said.

54. Diana was a music major in college.

55. When Hanson was working on *Middle of Nowhere* they rented a house in the Hollywood Hills.

56. Just before Hanson went off for their first promotional tour for Mercury Records, they stayed in the old Tulsa Little Theater for a week — just to practice.

57. Zac made a confession to MTV: "I think it's probably actually that I'm so shy, that I just act wacky to make up [for it]."

58. Hanson loves to shop at The Gap.

59. A week after Ike got his guitar, Zac got his drums, and Taylor got his keyboards, they performed!

60. The Dust Brothers helped produce Beck's *Odelay* CD, which impressed Ike and Taylor. Zac thought it was cool that Beck's last name is Hansen — "The Dust Brothers only work with people with the last name Hanson," he kidded. (Even if they aren't spelled the same!)

61. Hanson told *Time for Kids* they practice four hours a day.

62. Ike has his driver's license.
63. Ike, Tay, and Zac love to play Laser Quest.
64. The boys used to sing "Amen" after grace at the dinner table.
65. One of Hanson's favorite Tulsa restaurants is Rex's Boneless Chicken.
66. Zac's birthday is October 22, 1985.
67. Ike's birthday is November 17, 1980.
68. Zac is a Libra.
69. Ike is a Scorpio.
70. Zac says that "everyday life" inspires him to write songs.
71. Zac's favorite color is blue.
72. Ike's favorite color is green.
73. Zac told *Teen Beat* the first thing he does when he goes home is "Sleep!"
74. Taylor told *BOP* that Zac is very smart. "He's good at English. He read *Romeo & Juliet* and *Hamlet*." Ike added, "A lot of people don't read that until high school."
75. Ike wears a silver ring on the middle finger of his left hand.